Paddington Bear

MICHAEL BOND

ILLUSTRATED BY R.W. ALLEY

First published in hardback by HarperCollins *Publishers*, USA in 1988.
First published in Great Britain in hardback by Collins in 1998. First published in Picture Lions in 1999
Picture Lions is an imprint of the Children's Division, part of HarperCollins*Publishers* Ltd
77-85 Fulham Palace Road, Hammersmith, London, W6 8JB
The HarperCollins website address is www.fireandwater.com
7 9 8 6
Text copyright © Michael Bond 1998. Illustrations copyright © R.W. Alley 1998.
ISBN 0 00 771117 4
Manufactured in Thailand for Imago

An imprint of HarperCollins*Publishers*

Mr and Mrs Brown first met Paddington on a railway platform. In fact, that was how he came to have such an unusual name for a bear, because Paddington was the name of the station.

The Browns were waiting to meet their daughter, Judy, when Mr Brown noticed something small and furry half hidden behind some bicycles. "It looks like a bear," he said.

"A bear?" repeated Mrs Brown. "In Paddington station? Don't be silly, Henry. There can't be!"

But Mr Brown was right. It was sitting on an old leather suitcase marked WANTED ON VOYAGE, and as they drew near it stood up and politely raised its hat.

"Good afternoon," it said. "May I help you?"

"That's very kind of you," said Mr Brown, "but as a matter of fact, we were wondering if we could help *you*?"

"You're a very small bear to be all alone in a station," said Mrs Brown. "Where are you from?"

The bear looked around carefully before replying.

"Darkest Peru. I'm not really supposed to be here at all.
I'm a stowaway."

"You don't mean to say you've come all the way from South America by yourself?" exclaimed Mrs Brown. "Whatever did you do for food?"

Unlocking the suitcase with a small key, the bear took out an almost empty glass jar. "I ate marmalade," it said. "Bears like marmalade."

Mrs Brown took a closer look at the label around the bear's neck. It said, quite simply,

PLEASE LOOK AFTER THIS BEAR. Thank you.

"Oh, Henry!" she cried. "We can't just leave him here. There's no knowing what might happen to him. Can't he come home and stay with us?"

"Stay with us?" repeated Mr Brown nervously. He looked down at the bear. "Er, would you like that?" he asked. "That is," he added hastily, "if you have nothing else planned."

"Oooh, yes," replied the bear. "I would like that very much. I've nowhere to go and everyone seems in such a hurry."

"That settles it," said Mrs Brown. "Now, you must be thirsty after your journey. Mr Brown will buy you a nice cup of tea while I go and meet our daughter, Judy."

"But, Mary," said Mr Brown. "We don't even know his name."

Mrs Brown thought for a moment. "I know," she said. "We can call him Paddington! After the station."

"Paddington!" The bear tested it several times to make sure. "It sounds very important."

Mr Brown tried it out next. "Follow me, Paddington," he said. "I'll take you to the restaurant."

Paddington had never been inside a restaurant before, and he was very excited when he saw what Mr Brown had bought him.

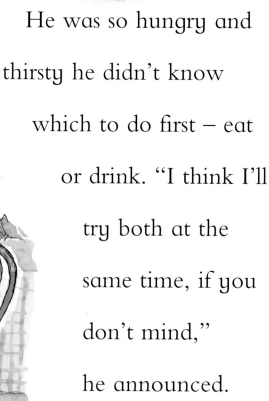

He was so hungry and thirsty he didn't know which to do first – eat or drink. "I think I'll try both at the same time, if you don't mind," he announced.

Without waiting for a reply, he climbed up onto the table and promptly stepped on a large cream and jam cake.

Mr Brown stared out of the window, pretending he had tea with a bear in Paddington station every day of his life.

"Henry!" cried Mrs Brown, when she arrived with Judy. "What are you doing to that poor bear? He's covered in jam and cream."

Paddington jumped up to raise his hat. In his haste, he slipped on a patch of strawberry jam and fell over backwards into his cup of tea.

"I think we'd better go before anything else happens," said Mr Brown.

Judy took hold of Paddington's paw. "Come along," she said. "We'll take you home and you can meet Mrs Bird and my brother, Jonathan."

Mr Brown led the way to a waiting taxi. "Number thirty-two Windsor Gardens, please," he said.

The driver stared at Paddington. "Bears is extra. Sticky bears is twice as much. And make sure none of it comes off on my interior. It was clean when I set out this morning."

The Browns climbed into the back of the taxi and

Paddington stood on a little tip-up seat behind the driver

so that he could see where they were going.

The sun was shining as they drove out of the station, and
there were cars and big red buses everywhere. Paddington
waved to some people waiting at a bus stop, and several
of them waved back. One man even raised his hat. It was
all very friendly.

Paddington tapped the taxi driver on the shoulder. "It isn't a bit like Darkest Peru," he announced.

The man jumped at the sound of Paddington's voice. "Cream!" he said bitterly. "All over me new coat!" There was a bang as he slid the little window behind him shut.

"Oh dear, Henry," murmured Mrs Brown. "I wonder if we're doing the right thing?"

Fortunately, before anyone had time to answer, they arrived at Windsor Gardens. Judy helped Paddington out of the taxi, and together they went up some steps towards a green front door.

"Now you're going to meet Mrs Bird," said Judy. "She looks after us. She's a bit fierce at times, but she doesn't really mean it. I'm sure you'll like her."

Paddington peered at his reflection in the brightly polished letterbox.

"I'm sure I shall, if you say so," he replied. "The thing is, will she like me?"

"Goodness gracious!" exclaimed Mrs Bird. "What *have* you got there?"

"It's not a what," said Judy. "It's a bear. His name's Paddington, and he's coming to stay with us."

"A bear," said Mrs Bird, as Paddington raised his hat. "Well, he has good manners, I'll say that for him."

"I'm afraid I stepped in some cream cakes by mistake," said Paddington.

"I can see that," said Mrs Bird. "I'd better get Jonathan to run a bath. I daresay you'll be wanting some marmalade, too!"

"I think she likes you," whispered Judy.

While Jonathan ran the water,
Judy gave Paddington some
soap and a towel.

But Paddington was much
too busy to bother with either.

First, he tried writing his
name in the steam on the mirror.
Then he used Mr Brown's
shaving cream to draw a map
of Peru on the floor.

It wasn't until a drip landed on his head that he
remembered he was supposed to be having a bath.

He soon discovered that wasn't as easy as it sounded.

It's one thing getting into a bath, but quite another matter

getting out again – especially when the tub

is full of water and your

eyes are covered

in soap.

Paddington tried calling out "Help!" – at first in a very quiet voice

so as not to disturb anyone, then very loudly, "HELP! HELP!"

When that didn't work, he began baling the water out with his

hat. But the hat had several holes in it, and his map of Peru soon

turned into a sea of foam.

Suddenly, Jonathan and Judy burst into the bathroom and lifted a dripping Paddington onto the floor.

"Thank goodness you're all right!" cried Judy.

"Fancy making all this mess," said Jonathan admiringly. "Even I've never made as much mess as this! But why didn't you just pull the plug out?"

"Oh," said Paddington. "I never thought of that."

When Paddington came downstairs, he looked so clean
no one could possibly be cross with him. His fur was all soft
and silky, his nose gleamed and his
paws had lost all traces of
the jam and cream.

The Browns made room for him in a small armchair by
the fire, and Mrs Bird brought him a pot of tea and a
plate of hot buttered toast.

"Now," said Mrs Brown, "you must tell us all about yourself. I'm sure you must have had lots of adventures."

"I have," said Paddington earnestly. "Things are always happening to me. I'm that sort of a bear." He settled back in his armchair and stretched out his toes towards the fire.

"I was brought up by my Aunt Lucy in Darkest Peru," he began. "But then she had to go into a Home for Retired Bears in Lima." He closed his eyes thoughtfully and a hush fell over the room as everyone waited expectantly.

After a while, when nothing happened, they

began to get restless. Mr Brown coughed loudly, then

he reached across and poked Paddington with his finger.

"Well, I never," said Mr Brown. "I do believe he's fast asleep!"

"Are you surprised?" asked Mrs Brown.